Published simultaneously in Canada. Manufactured in China by RR Donnelley Asia Printing Solutions Ltd.
Designed by Marikka Tamura. Text set in Catchup and Comic Sans. The art was done in pencil and watercolor.
Library of Congress Cataloging-in-Publication Data
Orloff, Karen Kaufman. I wanna iguana / Karen Kaufman Orloff ; illustrated by David Catrow.   p. cm.
Summary: Alex and his mother write notes back and forth in which Alex tries to persuade her to let him have a baby iguana for a pet.
[1. Iguanas as pets—Fiction. 2. Pets—Fiction. 3. Letters—Fiction. 4. Mothers and sons—Fiction.] I. Catrow, David, ill.
II. Title. PZ7.O6332 Iw 2004 [E]—dc21   2002010895
ISBN 978-0-399-23717-1

To Max and Emily
for their inspiration,
to Brad for his support,
and to all my writer friends
for making me work harder. —K.K.O.

To Mr. Alexander—
you taught me discipline
and how to be an artist. —D.C.

Dear Mom,
I know you don't think I should
have Mikey Gulligan's baby iguana
when he moves, but here's why I should.
If I don't take it, he goes to Stinky and
Stinky's dog, Lurch, will eat it.
You don't want that to happen, do you?
Signed,
Your sensitive son,
Alex

Dear Alex,

I'm glad you're so compassionate,
but I doubt that Stinky's mother
will let Lurch get into
the iguana's cage.
Nice try, though.

Love,
Mom

SEE!?

Dear Mom,
Did you know that iguanas are really quiet and they're cute too. I think they are much cuter than hamsters.

Love,
Your adorable son,
Alex

Dear Alex,
Tarantulas are quiet too, but I wouldn't want one as a pet. By the way, that iguana of Mikey's is uglier than Godzilla. Just thought I'd mention it.

Love,
Mom

Dear Mom,
You would never even have to see the iguana. I'll keep his cage in my room on the dresser next to my soccer trophies. Plus, he's so small, I bet you'll never even know he's there.

Love and a zillion and one kisses,
Alex

Dear Alex,
Iguanas can grow to be over six feet long. You won't have enough space in your whole room, much less on your dresser (with or without your trophies).
Love,
Mom

Dear Alex,

How are you going to get a girl to marry you when you own a six-foot-long reptile?

Love,

Your concerned mother

This iguana can be the brother I've always wanted.
Love,
Your lonely child, Alex

Dear Mom,
I know I have a brother but he's just a baby. What fun is that? If I had an iguana, I could teach it tricks and things. Ethan doesn't do tricks. He just burps and poops.
Love,
Grossed-out Alex

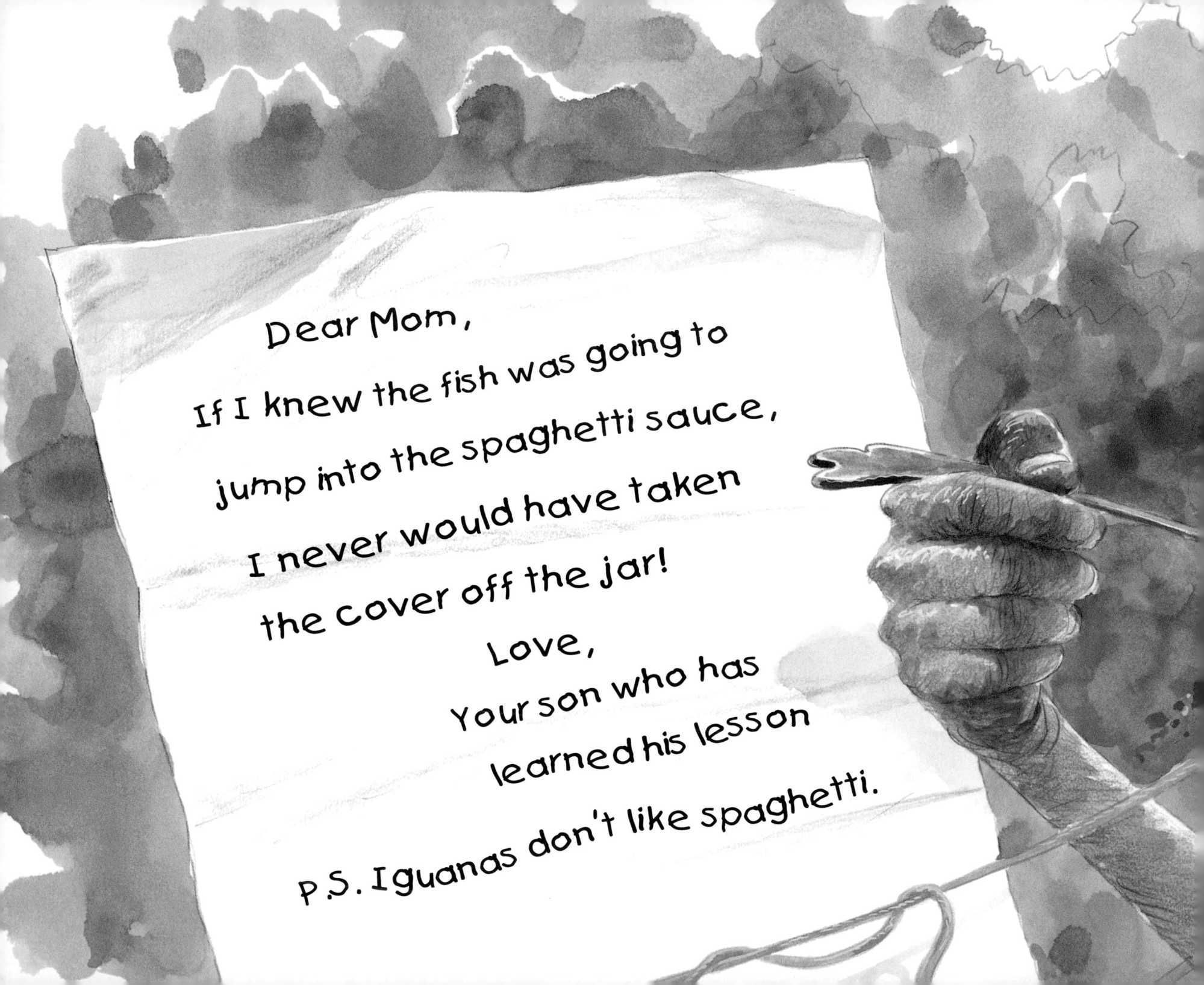

Dear Mom,

If I knew the fish was going to jump into the spaghetti sauce, I never would have taken the cover off the jar!

Love,
Your son who has learned his lesson

P.S. Iguanas don't like spaghetti.

Dear Mom,
I would feed him every day (he eats lettuce). And I would make sure he had enough water. And I would clean his cage when it got messy.
Love,
Responsible Alex
P.S. What's a trial basis?

Dear Alex,
A trial basis means Dad and I see how well you take care of him for a week or two before we decide if you can have him forever. Remember, Stinky and Lurch are waiting!
Love,
Mom

P.S. If you clean his cage as well as you clean your room, you're in trouble.

Dear Mom,
I'll really, really, really try to clean my room and the iguana's cage. Also, listen to this. I'll pay for the lettuce with my allowance. I mean, how much can one baby iguana eat, anyway?
Love,
Alex the financial wizard

"Are you sure you want to do this, Alex?"

"Yes, Mom!
I wanna iguana....
Please!"

Dear Alex,

Look on your dresser.

Love,

Mom